GOOD GAME

A SESAME STREET GUIDE TO BEING A GOOD SPORT

Charlotte Reed

Lerner Publications ◆ Minneapolis

In this guide, Elmo, Big Bird, Abby Cadabby, and their friends from *Sesame Street* learn what it means to be a good sport! Along the way, kids will be introduced to the importance of teamwork, following the rules, playing fair, and trying their best. With examples and prompts, this guide offers skills to help readers become smarter, stronger, and kinder.

Sincerely,

The Editors at Sesame Workshop

TABLE OF CONTENTS

INTRODUCTION

It's fun to play games! When you play with others, be a good sport.

WHAT IS A GOOD SPORT?

When you play fair, that means you're being a good sport. You follow the rules.

7

When you're being a good sport, you try your best. You're always willing to learn.

8

What was the last game
you played?

A good sport makes sure that everyone is included. Everybody should have the chance to play and feel welcome.

11

You can be a good sport by encouraging others. You can cheer for your teammates when they catch a ball.

If someone falls down, you can be a good sport by helping them up.

When you play together on a team, you work together. That's called teamwork.

How are you a
good teammate?

Sometimes, you'll win. Be proud that you won, and be kind to the other person or team.

When I win a game of checkers with Ernie, I always ask if he wants to play again.

Sometimes, you'll lose. It's okay to feel sad, but be a good sport and congratulate the other team.

When a game is over, you can say, "Good game!" This is a way to show kindness and be a good sport.

You can be a good sport in many ways.
A good sport plays with respect.

Name some ways you can be a good sport.

Being a good sport helps make games fun for everyone. Try your best, play fair, and treat everyone with kindness.

Elmo is ready to be a good sport with his friends on Sesame Street!

WHAT WOULD YOU DO?

If your team loses a game, what would you say to your team? What would you say to the team that won?

GLOSSARY

congratulate: to celebrate when someone else wins

respect: treating other people the way they want to be treated

rules: guidelines of a game that help make it safe and fun

teamwork: working together

READ MORE

Colella, Jill. *Keep Trying with Abby: A Book about Persistence*. Minneapolis: Lerner Publications, 2021.

Peters, Katie. *Playing Fair*. Minneapolis: Lerner Publications, 2022.

Rains, Dalton. *Sportsmanship*. Mendota Heights, MN: Little Blue House, 2023.

PHOTO ACKNOWLEDGMENTS

Image credits: HappyKids/E+/Getty Images, p. 4; monkeybusinessimages/iStock/Getty Images, pp. 6, 10; RonTech2000/iStock/Getty Images, p. 9; Lopolo/Shutterstock, p. 13; nirat/iStock/Getty Images, p. 14; Wavebreakmedia/iStock/Getty Images, p. 17; Giselleflissak/E+/Getty Images, p. 18; SDI Productions/E+/Getty Images, p. 21; pixdeluxe/E+/Getty Images, p. 22; LSOphoto/iStock/Getty Images, p. 25; PeopleImages/iStock/Getty Images, p. 26; bonniej/iStock/Getty Images, p. 28.

INDEX

To the Reynolds family, in honor of game night

Lerner Publications Company
An imprint of Lerner Publishing Group, Inc.
241 First Avenue North
Minneapolis, MN 55401 USA

For reading levels and more information, look up this title at www.lernerbooks.com.

Main body text set in MIkado.
Typeface provided by HvD Fonts.

Editor: Amber Ross **Designer:** Emily Harris
Photo Editor: Annie Zheng
Lerner team: Martha Kranes

Library of Congress Cataloging-in-Publication Data

Names: Reed, Charlotte, 1997- author.
Title: Good game : a Sesame Street guide to being a good sport / Charlotte Reed.
Description: Minneapolis, MN : Lerner Publications, [2024] | Includes bibliographical references and index. | Audience: Ages 4–8 years | Audience: Grades K-1 | Summary: "Sometimes you win, sometimes you lose. Join Elmo, Abby, and their Sesame Street friends to learn what it means to be a good sport"— Provided by publisher.
Identifiers: LCCN 2023031904 (print) | LCCN 2023031905 (ebook) | ISBN 9798765620212 (lib. bdg.) | ISBN 9798765629192 (pbk.) | ISBN 9798765636084 (epub)
Subjects: LCSH: Sportsmanship–Juvenile literature. | Sesame Street (Television program)
Classification: LCC GV706.3 .R436 2024 (print) | LCC GV706.3 (ebook) | DDC 175–dc23/eng/20230925

LC record available at https://lccn.loc.gov/2023031904
LC ebook record available at https://lccn.loc.gov/2023031905

Manufactured in the United States of America
1-1010249-51826-11/1/2023